Pokémon BW RIVAL DESTINIES

BATTLE FOR THE BOLT BADGE

Adapted by Simcha Whitehill from the episode "Dazzling the Nimbasa Gym!"

ISBN 978-0-545-40319-1

© 2012 Pokémon. © 1997-2012 Nintendo, Creatures, GAME FREAK, TV Tokyo, ShoPro, JR Kikaku. TM, ® Nintendo.
All Rights Reserved.
Published by Scholastic Inc.
SCHOLASTIC and associated logos are trademarks and/or registered trademarks of Scholastic Inc.

12 11 10 9 8 7 6 5 4 3 2 1   12 13 14 15 16 17/0

Designed by Cheung Tai
Printed in the U.S.A.   40
First printing, September 2012

SCHOLASTIC INC.

Ash, Pikachu, and their friends Iris and Cilan were visiting Nimbasa City.

LET'S SEE. ELESA'S ZEBSTRIKA USES *ELECTRIC-TYPE* MOVES. . . .

Ash was busy planning his battle strategy against the Nimbasa City Gym Leader, Elesa. He was determined to win his next Unova Gym badge.

ALL RIGHT, IT'S TIME!

THE ONLY WAY TO GET INSIDE THE NIMBASA CITY GYM WAS BY RIDING A ROLLERCOASTER.

AAAAAAH!

WHEEEEE!

PIKACHUUUUUUUUUUU!

ASH'S TRUSTY YELLOW POKÉMON WAS SITTING THIS BATTLE OUT.

COME HERE, PIKACHU!

ASH! I'VE BEEN WAITING FOR YOU.

ASH STEPPED INTO THE STADIUM. THERE WAS A HUGE CROWD THERE TO WATCH THE BATTLE.

THE THREE-ON-THREE BATTLE WAS ABOUT TO BEGIN!

ELESA'S ZEBSTRIKA BURST OUT OF ITS POKÉ BALL.

FEEL THE **SPARK!** AND FEEL THE **TINGLE!** WATCH ME MIX AND MINGLE!

ZEBSTRIKA: THE THUNDERBOLT POKÉMON

ZEBSTRIKKKKKA!

I CHOOSE *YOU,* PALPITOAD!

ASH'S POKÉMON WAS READY TO BATTLE.

PALPITOAD!

PALPITOAD: THE VIBRATION POKÉMON

ASH DECIDED TO MAKE THE FIRST MOVE.

PALPITOAD, USE MUD SHOT!

PALPITOAD FIRED OFF A ROUND OF BROWN DIRT BALLS.

PALP PALP PALP!

BUT SPEEDY ZEBSTRIKA DODGED THE MOVE.

NOW, FLAME CHARGE!

ZEBSTRIKA RACED ACROSS THE BATTLEFIELD.

BUT ITS FIERY ATTACK HAD NO EFFECT ON A WATER- AND GROUND-TYPE LIKE PALPITOAD.

ELESA HAD ANOTHER TRICK UP HER SLEEVE. . . .

ZEBSTRIKA, DOUBLE KICK!

FLAME CHARGE HAD POWERED UP ZEBSTRIKA. NOW IT HAD SUPERSPEED.

THE ATTACK HIT! PALPITOAD WAS DAZED.

PAA-AAA-AAALP. . . .

NOW PALPITOAD WAS READY TO MAKE ITS MOVE. . . .

SUPERSONIC!

THEN ASH HAD AN IDEA FOR A WINNING COMBINATION — MUD SHOT AND HYDRO PUMP!

PALPI-TOA-OA-OA-OA!

WAY TO GO, PALPITOAD!

SPLASH!

WITH THAT, ASH AND PALPITOAD WON THE FIRST ROUND!

A BRILLIANT COMEBACK!

AWESOME! PALPITOAD DID IT!

BUT THE MATCH WASN'T OVER YET. ELESA BROUGHT OUT HER SECOND POKÉMON.

ALL RIGHT, EMOLGA! THE BRIGHT LIGHT'S ON YOU!

EMOLGA: THE SKY SQUIRREL POKÉMON

EMO, EMO!

EMOLGA ZOOMED IN WITH ACROBATICS.

EMOOOOLLLLLLLGA!

PALPI?

PALPITOAD TRIED TO SQUEAK OUT SUPERSONIC, BUT IT WAS TIRED.

PAAAAAAAAAAL. . . .

EMOLGA USED ONE OF ITS TRICKIEST MOVES — ATTRACT.

WINK!

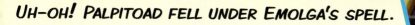

UH-OH! PALPITOAD FELL UNDER EMOLGA'S SPELL.

ASH DIDN'T KNOW WHAT TO DO NEXT. AND HE HAD TO PUT HIS SECOND POKÉMON INTO PLAY — FAST!

I CHOOSE *YOU*, SNIVY!

SNIVY: THE GRASS SNAKE POKÉMON

SNIVY!

SNIVY WAS TOUGH, BUT IT WASN'T THE BEST CHOICE FOR THIS BATTLE. . . .

HUH?

BUT EMOLGA SIMPLY FLEW AWAY, DODGING ALL OF SNIVY'S ATTACKS.

EMOLGA!

SNIVY, NO!

WATCHING THE BATTLE GOT PIKACHU ALL FIRED UP. IT WANTED TO JUMP IN AND HELP OUT!

PIKAAAAAA!

EMOLGA SEEMED TO BE COMING FROM EVERYWHERE AT ONCE!

SNIVY WAS TOO TIRED TO KEEP BATTLING. ASH HAD LOST THE SECOND ROUND.

SNIVY! YOU OKAY? YOU DESERVE A GOOD REST!

THE FANS SEEMED TO THINK THE BATTLE WAS AS GOOD AS OVER . . .

GO, ELESA!

HOORAY!

YAY!

. . . BUT ASH STILL HAD ONE MORE CHANCE. IT WAS TIME TO PICK HIS THIRD AND FINAL POKÉMON.

WHAT AM I GONNA DO?! THERE'S *THIS* TYPE, AND THERE'S *THAT* TYPE, SO *NOW* WHAT?!

I THOUGHT I NEEDED TO THINK UP SOME SORT OF AWESOME PLAN BY MYSELF! BUT I **FORGOT** SOMETHING... I CAN'T BATTLE WITHOUT MY POKÉMON!

PIKA, PIKA!

I'M USELESS BY MYSELF. PIKACHU, I NEED YOUR **HELP**, BUDDY!

LET'S **BATTLE**. WHAT DO YOU SAY?

PIIIIIKAAAAA!

A BATTLE BETWEEN TWO ELECTRIC-TYPES IS A SHOW OF SPIRIT AND STRENGTH.

LET'S GIVE THEM A **CHARGE!**

PIKACHU BEGAN WITH A BLAST OF ELECTRO BALL!

PIKACHUUUUUUUUUU!

BUT EMOLGA COUNTERED WITH THE SAME MOVE!

ASH WAS THINKING FAST, AND PIKACHU ACTED EVEN FASTER.

YEAH! USE *QUICK ATTACK!*

EMO?!

PIKACHU WON THE ROUND AGAINST EMOLGA!

WHAT? EMOLGA!

ELESA HAD TO CHOOSE HER THIRD AND FINAL POKÉMON.

IT'S MY *TYNAMO!* THE BRIGHT LIGHT IS ON *YOU!*

TYNAMO: THE ELEFISH POKÉMON

TYNAMO!

I'D BETTER BE *SHARP!*

PIIIKAAA?

ASH LOOKED UP THE LITTLE ELECTRIC-TYPE IN HIS POKÉDEX.

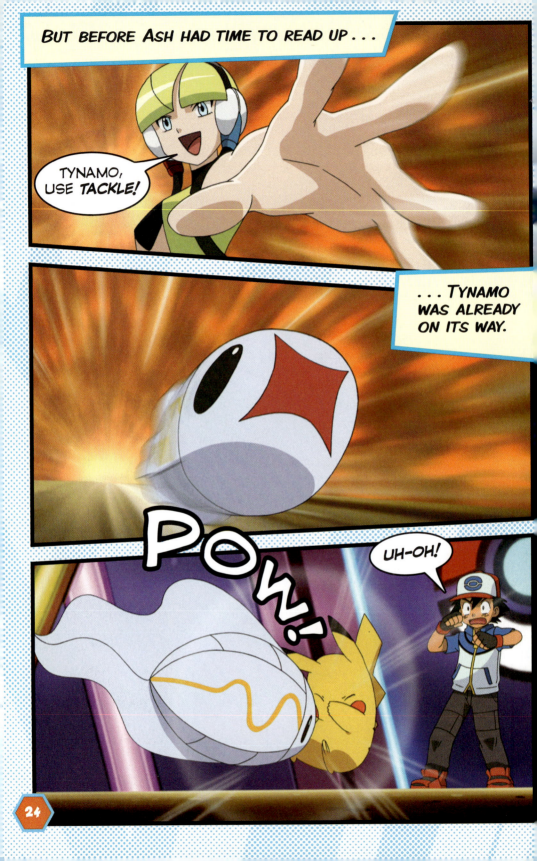

BAM!

THWAP!

Tynamo's Tackles pinned Pikachu to the ground!

I KNOW YOU CAN KEEP BATTLING, PIKACHU, *PLEASE!*

PIKACHU WORKED WITH ALL ITS MIGHT TO BREAK FREE.

PIIIIKKKAAAACHUUUUUU!

SOON THE LITTLE YELLOW POKÉMON WAS BACK ON TOP AND READY TO BATTLE!

PIKACHU WAS JUST IN TIME FOR ASH'S LATEST PLAN. . . .

PIKACHU, *THUNDERBOLT!* AND I WANT *TONS!*

PIKACHU CHARGED UP . . .

PIKAAAAAAAA . . .

. . . AND FIRED OFF BRIGHT BOLTS OF LIGHTNING!

. . . CHU-CHU-CHU!

ZAP!

ZAP!

ZAP!

27

HE KNOW **ELECTRIC-T** MOVES AREN EFFECTIVE ON TYNAMO!

ASH HAS A COMPLETELY **DIFFERENT** PLAN UP HIS SLEEVE!

BUT EVERYTHING SEEMED TO BE GOING ACCORDING TO ASH'S PLAN. . . .

AWESOME! KEEP UP THOSE **THUNDERBOLTS!**

ELESA DECIDED IT WAS TIME FOR HER TO MAKE HER MOVE.

WHAT COULD THEY BE UP TO?

YAY, YAY, **YAY!**

CONGRATULATIONS, ASH!

THANKS!

THANKS A LOT, PIKACHU!

PIKACHU!

It was time for Ash, Cilan, and Iris to say good-bye to their new pal Elesa.

The two of you make a **brilliant** team!

Wow, I finally got my fourth badge!

That's great, Ash!

Come on, Pikachu!

And with that, our heroes were on the road to their next adventure!